WHY DIDN'T YOU TELL ME?

Piccadilly Pips

WHY DIDN'T YOU TELL ME?

Hilary McKay
Illustrated by John Eastwood

Piccadilly Press • London

Phototypeset from author's disk by Piccadilly Press.
Printed and bound in India by Thomson Press
for the publishers Piccadilly Press Ltd.,
5 Castle Road, London NW1 8PR

A catalogue record for this book is available from the British
Library

ISBN: 1 85340 353 9 (hardback)
1 85340 425 X (paperback)

Hilary McKay lives in Derbyshire. She was joint winner of the 1992
Guardian Children's Fiction Award for
THE EXILES. This is her first book for Piccadilly Press.

John Eastwood lives in Brighton. He studied fine art at
Ravensbourne College of Art and has been illustrating for several
years. This is his first book for Piccadilly Press.

CHAPTER ONE

Nicholas Brown was eight years old. He had hair the colour of bonfire flames and freckles as big as raindrops. The gap where his two front teeth should have been had been a gap for so long that his friends could not imagine his face any other way.

He did not look the sort of boy who had mittens on strings through his coat sleeves. Or who, when party invitations arrived saying, *PLEASE WEAR OLD CLOTHES*, had no old clothes to wear. Or whose mother walked him to school every morning carrying his lunchbox (in case Nick held it the wrong way up) and kissed him goodbye right outside the school gates, in front of the lollipop lady and everyone.

But he was.

Nick had a best friend called Sam. He was such a good friend that he called for Nick every morning and walked to school with him and his mother, despite the daily risk of being kissed in front of the lollipop lady himself, which was what sometimes happened if Sam did not escape into the playground fast enough.

"You're going to have to stop her

doing that," said Sam, rejoining Nick one morning after having watched from a safe distance the dismal affair at the school gates. "That holding your hand to cross the road and the kissing anyway."

"I know," replied Nick. "I've tried. It's not easy."

It was a conversation they had often had but that day Miss Gilhoolie, their class teacher, happened to overhear as she crossed the playground.

"It's because you're a one and only, Nick!" she remarked.

"One and only what?" demanded Nick, but she had vanished into school.

"One and only what?" repeated Nick as soon as they got inside. "Line up for assembly and stop talking!" said Miss Gilhoolie.

"One and only what?" asked Nick (who was very persistent) when assembly was over and they were all streaming back to the classroom.

"What?" asked Miss Gilhoolie, "SAMUEL OLIVER I SAW THAT! Sorry Nick?"

"Because I'm a one and only what?" repeated Nick patiently.

"Oh," said Miss Gilhoolie, remembering, "child. The only one your mother has got! No wonder she doesn't want you squashed on the road!"

Nick thought this was not a reasonable thing to say. He thought of Sam and Mrs Oliver, and what she would say if Sam was squashed on the road.

"Oh never mind," he imagined Mrs Oliver saying. "I have plenty more. Three actually. It's not as if he was a one and only!"

Somehow this did not seem very likely. And what else was Miss Gilhoolie saying?

"It was just the same for me! I was an only child like you! Carted around everywhere for years and years and years."

"How many years?" asked Nick, wondering how much longer he had still to go and thinking that eight years' carting had been plenty long enough. "How many years? More than eight?"

"Eight?" laughed Miss Gilhoolie. "More like eighteen!"

"Another ten years?" asked Sam at lunchtime when Nick repeated this conversation to him. *"Another ten years!"*

"That's what Miss Gilhoolie said," Nick told him gloomily.

"Another ten years," said Sam. "Another *ten* years!"

"Don't keep saying it," said Nick.

"That'll be right through Big School," remarked Sam conversationally so Nick rugby-tackled his knees and their lunch boxes fell as they rolled together on the dining room floor.

"Another ten years!" gasped Sam, half choking on a mouthful of Nick's jumper. "That'll be right through Big Sch..."

"NICK AND SAM!" roared Miss Gilhoolie who was supervising

Packed Lunch Dinner. "GET UP!
PICK UP THAT FOOD! IF I SEE
YOU FIGHTING AGAIN…"

"It's all right Miss Gilhoolie," Sam
told her when Nick was no longer
sitting on his chest and he could
breathe again. "We weren't fighting."

"We were talking," added Nick,
collecting together his packet of

cheese and tomato sandwiches (labelled *"Eat First"*), his chocolate flapjack (labelled *"Eat If You Have Finished Your Sandwiches"*) and wiping up his homemade yoghurt with the paper napkin thoughtfully provided by his mother.

"Talking!" said Miss Gilhoolie.

"About the future," said Sam, gathering up half a pork pie, a handful of banana rusks and a jar of chocolate pudding (labelled *"Suitable for babies over six months"* – Sam was allowed to pack up his own lunches). "About the future, Miss Gilhoolie."

"Next lesson is games," said Miss Gilhoolie. "Any more bother from either of you and your futures will be sitting in the classroom while everyone else is outside!"

"Have a rusk," said Sam when she had gone. "They're strengthening! They give our twins strength anyway!"

"Mum never buys rusks," said Nick mournfully. "She says I'm too old. And for chocolate pudding."

"Tell her it's full of vitamins," said
Sam. "Look! It says so on the label."

"She'd rather make yoghurt."

"Another ten years of homemade
yoghurt," said Sam. "And being
taken to school and kissed in front of
the lollipop lady, and packed lunches
with labelled sandwiches! What you
need...Get off, Miss Gilhoolie's
looking... ! I wasn't being horrible I
was just saying! What you need, is a
baby."

"A baby?"

"Then you wouldn't be a one and only!"

"A baby!" repeated Nick, and wondered why he had never thought of it before.

CHAPTER TWO

"A baby?" said Nick's mother.

"Or two," said Nick. "Or three.
Mrs Oliver has three, besides Sam!"

"Mrs Oliver is a saint," said Nick's
mother.

"A baby?" asked Nick's father. "Do
you know what a baby would mean?
Half as much of everything!
Pushchairs in the hall. Crying at
night. Keeping quiet while it's
asleep..."

"It would be worth it," said Nick.

"Worth it?"

"Not to be a one and only."

"I always *wanted* to be a one and only," said Nick's father.

"You wouldn't have if you were one," said Nick.

Once Nick had got an idea into his head he wasn't the sort of person to forget it. Or to let anyone else forget it. Sam fell ill and was off school for a week and without him Nick felt more of a one and only than ever and redoubled his campaign to acquire a baby in the house.

After a few days of Nick's efforts his parents grew very weak and broke down to the point of saying, "Well you never know," and "Perhaps you're right," and "Well, we'll have to see."

After a few weeks they seemed to give up completely.

"Yes Nick," they said. "We have been thinking about it and you are quite right. But babies do not arrive all at once and it is early days yet."

"Early days for what?"

"To talk about me having a baby."

"Are you having a baby?" asked Nick.

"Well I hope so," said his mother cautiously. "One day."

"One day!" said Sam when Nick repeated this conversation.

"Don't you think it might be working?"

"When I ask if we can go on a safari holiday and whether I can have a television in my bedroom or anything like that they always say 'One day'" said Sam. "And one day never comes. Perhaps they're just saying it to shut you up. If you don't mind me saying, your mum is looking jolly thin; just look at her beside mine!"

Nick looked across the play-ground. There was his mother, almost eclipsed by large, rosy Mrs Oliver standing beside her.

"And don't forget the airport!" said Sam.

"Oh," said Nick, deflating

suddenly. "Oh yes."

The airport had been at the beginning of Nick and Sam's friendship. It had come about as the result of enormous pestering by Nick (backed up by Sam) and aimed at Nick's father. The subject

had been aeroplanes, and the sad fact
that Nick and Sam were the only
boys in their class never to have been
on one. Or even to have seen one,
close to. Or even to have visited an
airport. And at the end of the
pestering (which had lasted for
several hours) Nick's father had
grabbed both boys, stuffed them in
his car, driven them to the nearest
airport, parked them in window
seats over-looking the airfield with
instructions not to move, disappeared,
and returned with a flight schedule.

They had sat, temporarily silenced
by the combined fierceness and
amazing generosity of Nick's father,
and waited all afternoon for their
flight to be called. And at the end of
the afternoon Nick's father had said
proudly, "Now you can't say you've

never seen an aeroplane close to!"
and had driven them home, never
suspecting that he had not given
them a stunningly brilliant
afternoon. Which was why the boys
(especially Sam) were inclined to
regard all promises unsubstantiated
by hard proof as nothing but
Airport.

However, Nick had decided that life
as a one and only was not for him
and he did not give up.

"Airport," said Sam when he
described how one weekend the
attic had been visited and his old
cot rooted out. "Keep up the
pressure!"

"You were right," Nick told him a
week later. "They've forgotten that

cot already. It's stuck in my bedroom blocking off the window. They're painting the spare room yellow now. It would make a jolly good baby's room."

"You should have told them so."

"I did."

"What did they say?"

"They said, 'Yes it would'. But it's probably only all Airport again. Mum has washed my old Peter Rabbit curtains and hung them in the window."

"Do not let them shut you up so easily," advised Sam, gazing mean-ingfully at the thinness of Nick's mother.

"They've even hung up a mobile," said Nick, "and they leave catalogues with prams in lying about for me to find."

"They must think you're daft!" said Sam. "But don't give up! It will be worth it in the end!"

CHAPTER THREE

"Nick," said his mother. "About this baby."

"What baby?"

"The baby we talked about ages ago. You can't have forgotten! You must have seen us getting ready!"

"Peter Rabbit curtains and my old cot?"

"Yes," said his mother. "We shall be needing them again perhaps. I hope. After Christmas."

"After *Christmas*?" repeated Nick, very disappointed. For a moment his hopes had been raised, "But Christmas is ages away," he said.

"I suppose it is," agreed his mother. "And I didn't mean exactly straight after Christmas."

"After New Year?"

"Oh yes, after that."

"After we go back to school after New Year?"

"Oh yes. Probably after half-term actually."

"After Christmas after New Year after we go back to school next year. After we go back to school next year's *half-term*?"

"Yes," said his mother.

"Airport," said Sam. "Poor old Nick!"

"Yes," agreed Nick. "I suppose they think I'll have forgotten by then. Anything to shut me up!
My mum even dragged me into Boots to look at baby clothes on Saturday!"

"Well, keep it up," said Sam. "It's

either that or being a one and only and being run about after for the next ten years! Right through Big School! Poor old Nick!"

Christmas came closer and closer.

"Are they still doing it?" asked Sam. "Pretending about that baby to shut you up?"

"They haven't mentioned it lately," admitted Nick. "It's all Christmas talk now."

"Better ask again," said Sam.

"Are we still having that baby after Christmas?" asked Nick, looking sternly at his mother, who despite three winter jumpers was still noticeably thinner than Mrs Oliver.

"Of course," said his mother laughing. "Didn't we tell you ages

ago? Why do you think the spare
room is being turned into a nursery?
You're being a bit difficult Nick!"

"Me!" said Nick astonished.
"Did you eat your lunch?"
"All but the yoghurt," said Nick.

CHAPTER FOUR

Nick's mother went to see Mrs Oliver.

"He won't believe it," she told her. "What else can we do? We've told him! We've created a nursery in front of his eyes! He can't seem to accept it."

"Perhaps," said Sam's mother, "you should drop the subject for a while."

"They've definitely given up on that baby idea," reported Nick gloomily.

"It's completely off.
It was all Airport; just like we thought. It's nothing but where we'll go for the summer holidays now."

"Never mind," said Sam comfortingly. "You're coming to stop with us at half-term. And your mum *is* getting fatter!"

"She's still a lot thinner than yours," said Nick, refusing to be cheered. "And do you know what they bought at the supermarket last night? Nappies! They must think I'm crackers!"

"Nick," said his father as he drove Nick and his luggage to Sam's house on the first morning of half-term. "You do realise, don't you?"

"Realise what?"
Nick's father sighed but said

patiently, "This baby. It could arrive any time now you know."

"It's all right," said Nick kindly. "You don't have to keep it up Dad. I've given up the baby idea."

"Too late now old son." Mr Brown replied cheerfully.

"But I've been wondering. Couldn't we get a dog?"

"What?"

"I said, what about a dog?"

"Good grief!"

"It was just an idea," said Nick.

"Your dad," said Sam that afternoon, "is certainly stubborn! And your mum! Oh well, you will just have to make up your mind to be a one and only and run about after for the next ten years! That'll be right through Big School! Poor old Nick!"

"I'll give you Poor Old Nick!" exclaimed Mrs Oliver. "As soon as I get the twins and the baby to bed and have five minutes peace I'm going to have a word with Poor Old Nick!"

However, before Mrs Oliver was anywhere near getting five minutes peace Nick's father was back, banging on the front door.

Sam answered it.

"A boy! A boy!" shouted Nick's father. "Another boy! Where's Nick? I want him now! Straight away! At once!"

"But we've just laid all my track out upstairs," protested Sam. "You said he could stay! He's only just come!"

"Go and fetch Nick at once!" said Mrs Oliver. "Really Sam!"

"Your dad's here and he looks awful!" Sam told Nick. "What a mess! And he wants you straight away now at once. Might have known they'd never really let their one and only stop for half-term."

Nick's father drove the sulking Nick right across town. Right to the hospital. Marched him down miles

and miles of corridors, shoved him
through a swing door, led him to a
bed. His mother was in it, holding a
baby.

"Whose is it?" asked Nick,
thinking, "Will they stop at
nothing?"

"Ours!" shouted his father. "Ours! Yours! Your brother! Your new brother Michael! Look, he's even got a label on! Michael Brown!"

"What an awful shock!" said Sam.

"Yes," agreed Nick. "They gave him to me to hold and they said, 'Say something Nick!' They were all laughing, Mum, Dad, the people in the other beds, nurses. They even brought in extra nurses to laugh! And they kept saying, 'Say something Nick! Say something Nick!'"

"They kept it very secret," said Sam. "They must have known for weeks! Months! So what *did* you say?"

"I said, 'Why didn't you tell me? Why didn't you *tell* me? WHY DIDN'T YOU TELL ME?'"

"Poor old Nick," said Sam.

Other books in the series:

THE CAR-WASH WAR by Andrew Matthews
When Trees sets up a rival car-wash to her
brother, chaos breaks out as they find ever more
ingenious ways to win business!

DON'T LET IT RAIN by Yvonne Coppard
Ben is really looking forward to his birthday
party – there will be games and balloons and a
picnic in the park. But what if it rains?

JIMMY JELLY by Jacqueline Wilson
Angela likes Jimmy Jelly, the TV star, so much that
she has her *own* one, who only she can see. Then the
real Jimmy Jelly comes to the local shopping centre...

MISTER MAGGS by Helen Cresswell
Whenever Jemma does anything wrong, she
always blames it on "Mister Maggs".
Imagine her surprise when Mister Maggs
actually shows up!

THE MUCKITUPS by Robert Swindells
"The tidy, healthy, Hebridean Frimlys clash then mix with the junk-strewing, chain-smoking, telly-watching Muckitups!" – The Times

PRESS PLAY by Anne Fine
"...hilarious...will strike a chord with every parent" – Daily Telegraph